The Dead Sea Squirrels Series

Nutty Study Buddies

Mike Nawrocki

Illustrated by Luke Séguin-Magee

Tyndale House Publishers
Carol Stream, Illinois

Visit Tyndale's website for kids at tyndale.com/kids.

Visit the author's website at mikenawrocki.com.

TYNDALE is a registered trademark of Tyndale House Ministries. The Tyndale Kids logo is a trademark of Tyndale House Ministries.

The Dead Sea Squirrels is a registered trademark of Michael L. Nawrocki.

Nutty Study Buddies

Designed by Libby Dykstra

Edited by Sarah Rubio

Published in association with the literary agency of Brentwood Studios, 1550 McEwen, Suite 300 PNB 17, Franklin, TN 37067.

For manufacturing information regarding this product, please call 1-855-277-9400.

For information about special discounts for bulk purchases, please contact Tyndale House Publishers at csresponse@tyndale.com, or call 1-855-277-9400.

Library of Congress Cataloging-in-Publication Data
Names: Nawrocki, Michael, author.
Title: Nutty study buddies / Mike Nawrocki.
Description: Carol Stream, Illinois : Tyndale House Publishers, Inc., [2019]
  I Series: The Dead Sea squirrels I Summary: Michael learns that—like the
  Thessalonians in the Bible—he will prosper if he works hard when Pearl
  the 2,000-year-old squirrel helps him study for his math test.
Identifiers: LCCN 2018037976 I ISBN 9781496435064 (sc)
Subjects: I CYAC: Perseverance (Ethics)—Fiction. I Squirrels—Fiction. I Christian
  life—Fiction.
Classification: LCC PZ7.N185 Nu 2019 I DDC [Fic]—dc23 LC record available
  at https://lccn.loc.gov/2018037976

Printed in the United States of America

27   26   25   24   23   22   21
8   7   6   5   4   3

To my daughter, Alejandra (AKA Goose Juice)—
For all the hours we spent working through
math homework. I miss the hours
with you, but not the math.
Love, Dad

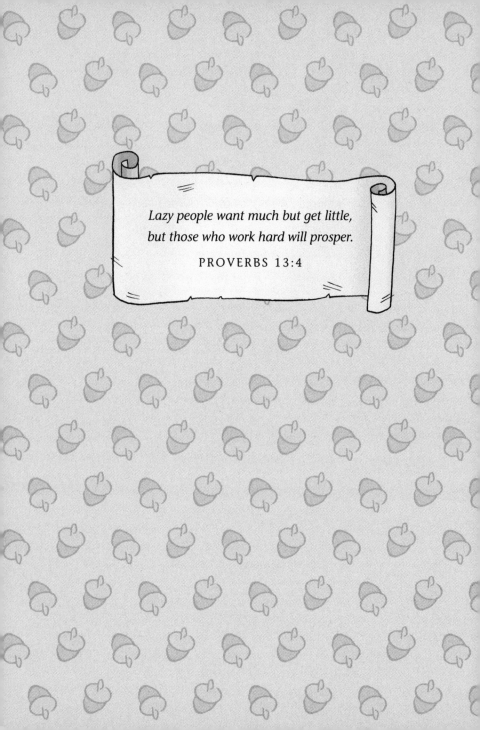

Lazy people want much but get little,
but those who work hard will prosper.

PROVERBS 13:4

He sets them up like posable action figures on his dresser—
under an open window.

While Michael is sleeping, a thunderstorm rolls in, and it begins to rain . . .

. . . rehydrating the squirrels!

Up and kicking again after almost 2,000 years, Merle and Pearl Squirrel have great stories and advice to share with the modern world.

They are the Dead Sea Squirrels!

CHAPTER 1

"Merle! Wake up, Merle!"

Merle Squirrel heard his wife, Pearl, calling him softly. He slowly opened his eyes to find himself surrounded by Pearl, Michael, Justin, and Sadie.

"What happened? Where am I?" Merle asked groggily. The last thing he remembered was being in the lunchroom of Walnut Creek Elementary School munching on a chicken nugget.

"We're back home, Merle," Michael said.

"I think my news was a little too much for you." Sadie smiled at him. Sadie had discovered that the squirrels had witnessed the Sermon on the

Mount firstpaw (which is like firsthand, except for squirrels), which meant that they must have been suspended in time in a cave by the Dead Sea for nearly 2,000 years. Merle and Pearl knew the world was much different now than the one they remembered, but knowing just how much time had passed had overwhelmed Merle.

"I didn't know squirrels could faint," Justin said. "I've seen goats do it." Justin stiffened his limbs and fell sideways onto the bed.

MAAAAA!

"You'd faint too if you realized you were 2,000 years old," Merle answered. "It's not natural. Squirrels usually go for a few decades, tops."

"We've got Methuselah beat by a long shot!" Pearl said proudly. "But we were asleep for most of it, so I'm not sure it counts for the record."

"This is huge, guys," Sadie said. "Michael, we need to tell your dad. He'll know what to do."

"No way!" Michael said. "I would get so busted. I just got done being grounded for getting lost in the cave. I don't know what Dad would do if he found out I smuggled back talking artifacts!"

"I resent being called an artifact." Merle sniffed. "Makes me feel old."

"You are old, dear." Pearl patted his paw.

"What if they have to go back to the Dead Sea?" Michael said.

"I don't wanna go back there!" Merle protested. "It's too hot!"

"We're not even from there. We were just on 'vacation,'" Pearl said, making air quotes with her paws.

"I like it here, where there are trees and nuts and chicken nuggets," Merle said. "Don't make us go back!"

"Nobody's making anybody go back."
Michael crossed his arms. "You can hide
out in my backpack. No one needs to
know."

"Michael," Sadie said, "they can't
hide in your backpack forever."

"No offense to your backpack," Pearl
agreed, "but it is a little snug."

5

"Well, Jane will be at school tomorrow, so maybe you guys can hang out in my room," Michael suggested. Michael's little sister, Jane, attended preschool three days a week. While she was at school, the family cat, Mr. Nemesis, stayed closed up in her room.

"Good idea," Merle said. "While you're at school tomorrow, we'll stay here and come up with a plan for where to settle down."

"Squirrel witness protection! It's like a spy movie!" Justin said. "I like it!"

"Well, we should get going, Justin," Sadie said. "We all have a math test to study for."

"Don't remind me!" Michael groaned as Sadie and Justin headed out.

CHAPTER 2

Math came much easier for Justin and Sadie than it did for Michael. For some reason, Michael had to study twice as hard to end up with the same grade.

"This stinks!" Michael complained as he sat at his desk, staring down at his math book. "I just don't get this. Why don't I get this?!"

"Let's have a look." Pearl hopped up onto Michael's desk. Pearl, a first-century rodent, was not schooled in formal mathematics. But she'd had to deal with limited resources her whole life, so she had a natural talent for counting and calculating. She peered at Michael's math book. "Hmm . . .

this looks interesting. I think I might be able to figure this out."

KNOCK, KNOCK, KNOCK! Someone rapped on Michael's door. Merle and Pearl looked at him in panic.

"Hide!" he whispered. The two squirrels scurried under Michael's bed as he called out, "Come in!"

"Hey, buddy!" Dr. Gomez, Michael's dad, opened the door. "What are you up to?"

Michael looked down at his math book. "Math," he said gloomily. "I have a test in a couple days."

"Not your favorite subject, huh?" Dr. Gomez asked.

"Not by a long shot. It's easy for Justin and Sadie. It's totally not fair."

"Well, some things come easier for some people. That just means you have to work a little harder."

"Like I said, totally not fair." Michael scowled.

"Tell you what," Dr. Gomez said, taking out his wallet. "Here's a little motivation." He pulled out a $10 bill. "If you can get at least a B on your test, this is for you. I'll stick it to the fridge."

"Make sure it's high enough so Jane can't snag it," Michael said.

Dr. Gomez smiled. "You're a smart kid. If you work hard, I'm sure you can get a good grade."

"Thanks, Dad."

Dr. Gomez ruffled Michael's hair. "Well, I'll leave you to it. Let me know if you need any help!" He left the room, calling over his shoulder, "If you need inspiration, check out the fridge!"

Pearl and Merle came out of hiding. "Well, you heard the man!" Pearl said, hopping back up onto Michael's desk.

"Ten dollars is a lot of money," Michael said. "Let's do this!"

But Michael's enthusiasm for studying didn't last longer than 10 minutes.

"Arrrgh!!!" Michael covered his face with his hands. "I don't get it!"

"Let me see if I can help you figure it out," Pearl said.

Michael slammed his math book shut. "I need a break. I'll do this tomorrow."

CHAPTER 3

Pearl scurried along the thick branch
of the walnut tree outside of Michael's
room, carrying a sack of walnuts.
She jumped down onto the windowsill and called out, "Merle! Breakfast!"
Walnuts were plentiful at that time
of year, so it hadn't taken her long to
find enough nuts for breakfast, lunch,
and dinner. She climbed into the room
and looked around for Merle. "Hello?"
she called out.

"Ahhhhh! Good morning!" Merle
sighed cheerfully as he exited Michael's
bathroom, wiping his wet whiskers with
the back of his paw. "It's incredible!
No matter how much I drink, it keeps

filling itself back up! I tell you, Pearl, it's like the loaves and the fishes!"

A few days earlier, Merle had discovered an inexhaustible source of water in Michael's bathroom. Merle had been so excited that Michael hadn't had the heart to tell him what a toilet is supposed to be used for.

The bedroom door burst open, and Michael ran in. "Hey, guys, gotta go! Justin's here!" He scurried for his backpack. For Justin, being on time to school meant getting there 30 minutes early. Being late totally freaked Justin out, which totally stressed Michael out. The result was two fifth graders who were always on time, which was a positive as far as their parents and teachers were concerned. "Have a great day, and figure out a good plan!" Michael called as he rushed out the door. Pearl noticed that his math book was still on the desk, but before she could remind him to take it, he shouted, "Make sure you keep the door closed in case Mr. Nemesis gets out! Bye!" And with that, he shut the door.

"You forgot your math book!" Pearl called, but Michael was gone.

MATH IS YOUR FRIEND
5TH GRADE EDITION

CHAPTER 4

"How's he going to study for his test without his book?" Pearl worried.

"Too late now." Merle hopped up on the desk and tried to lift the book. "There's no way we can bring this to his school—it's way too heavy!"

Suddenly, Pearl had an idea. "What if I work on figuring out how to help Michael with his test while you work on a plan for where we're going to live?" she asked Merle.

Merle knew that his job was going to be much more adventurous. "Sounds good to me! You explore the book, and I'll explore the trees!" he responded. As Pearl cracked open *Math Is Your Friend: 5th Grade Edition*, Merle scurried up a branch of the walnut tree outside Michael's bedroom.

When it comes to house hunting, the first thing a squirrel will look for is a nice hole in a tree, preferably somewhere up high. "High and dry!" as Merle liked to say. Squirrels aren't hole makers, just hole finders. The two best bets are a knot that has fallen out or a decomposed area between branches. If a squirrel has no luck finding space inside a tree, they will resort to making space on the tree in the form of a nest. However,

18

nests are rarely as dry and cozy as a knothole. "If it's not a knot—not!" Merle also liked to say.

The good news about most of the trees near Michael's house was that they had plenty of knotholes. The bad news, as Merle found time after time, was that they were all occupied.

"AHHHHH!" screamed one squirrel.

"Sorry, miss!" Merle apologized.

"Who are you?!" demanded another.

"Beg your pardon, sir," Merle said.

"Get off my limb!" ordered a third.

HOME
SWEET
HOME

After a number of other awkward moments, and having grown tired and embarrassed of surprising other rodents in their homes, Merle headed back to Michael's bedroom. "Sorry, Pearl, there's no room in the inns," he reported.

"I figured as much," Pearl mumbled as she studied an explanation of long division. "Where there's a lot of nuts, there's bound to be a lot of squirrels."

"Those trees are definitely full of nuts," Merle agreed. No sooner had the words left his mouth than he noticed something interesting on the floor of Michael's room. "What's that?" he asked.

Pearl looked down and spotted what you or I would call an air vent. However, neither Merle nor Pearl had ever seen one. She shrugged and continued with her reading.

"It looks like a little jail in the ground." Merle approached the vent, noting the little metal bars that stretched across it. "I wonder what they keep in it?"

Not being a ground squirrel, Merle would normally have had no interest in exploring a damp, dirty hole in the ground as a potential home, especially one housing a potential prisoner. But this particular hole was dry and relatively clean. He grabbed the grate and easily lifted it off the floor. "If it is a jail, it's not a very good one," Merle remarked. "Pearl, I'm gonna check this out."

"That's nice, dear," Pearl answered softly, concentrating on her reading.

22

CHAPTER 5

"Time for math!" Ms. McKay called out. "Take out your books!"

Michael reached into his backpack and felt around for his math book. Then he unzipped the pack and looked inside. "Oh no!" he said.

"Is there something wrong, Michael?" Ms. McKay asked.

"Umm . . . no, ma'am," Michael answered, looking up from his pack. Ms. McKay turned to write on the smart board, and Michael leaned over to Justin. "I forgot my book. Can I look at yours?" he whispered.

"Sure." Justin slid his book to the edge of his desk.

Less than 10 minutes into the lesson, Michael got tired of listening to Ms. McKay while leaning over to read Justin's book, so he did what

TO BOOKSHELF →

← TO WINDOWS ←

many kids who are pretending to pay attention in class do—he doodled. By 30 minutes into the lesson, he'd sketched a masterpiece of plastic pipery: an intricate tangle of tubes running all over his bedroom, like the Taj Mahal for hamsters.

→ TO BATHROOM

FOOD STORAGE POD

25

SLEEPING POD

"Check this out," Michael whispered proudly to Justin, sliding his drawing over to his friend. "Merle and Pearl would love to live in something like this."

Justin was confused. "Michael, you do know that we have a test tomorrow? You've got to know this stuff!"

"I know, I know," Michael said. "I'll study when I get home."

CHAPTER 6

"Hello!" Merle called out into the pitch-black aluminum tunnel, his voice echoing off the metallic walls. He felt a sudden twinge of panic as he remembered being lost in the cave near the Dead Sea. Some memories, even ones that are 2,000 years old, don't fade easily. "What am I doing down here?!" he said to himself. He turned around and shouted, "Pearl, can you hear me?!"

27

"Right here," Pearl's slightly annoyed voice answered faintly. She was much more interested in her book than she was in what Merle was up to, but just hearing her voice helped to reassure him that he was not lost.

Suddenly, a very fast and very cold wall of air hit Merle head-on. "Whoa!" he yelled. "It's dark, cold, and windy, Pearl! This may not be the home we're looking for!" The rapid movement of the air carried Merle's voice clearly to Pearl, but she chose not to answer. But even if she had, her voice would not have carried back upstream. Though he didn't realize it, Merle was experiencing modern air-conditioning. "It's like winter down here!" he yelled. But just as he was about to give up and turn back toward Michael's room, he spotted a faint light up ahead. "What's that?" He pressed on through the frigid headwind.

After making his way forward a few more yards, Merle found himself looking up through another set of metal bars into a room above. With a little effort, he was able to push the grate up and out into the room. *Definitely not a jail*, he concluded, popping his head up into the room.

Merle found himself in a new world, one very different from Michael's room. This was a very pink world with lots of pillows. So, so many pillows. Merle crawled up out of the vent onto the floor, looking at walls lined with princess posters and a bookshelf full of dolls. "It's so . . . fluffy," he said out loud as he made his way into the center of the room. "Not exactly my

style, but very comfortable." Merle was
beginning to feel proud of himself for
having discovered this amazing, fluffy
world under the ground. He wondered
if this was what he was missing out
on by not being a ground squirrel.
"Pearl is going to love this!" he said
as he turned to see a big, white, fluffy
bed in the corner. But his joy quickly

turned to terror when he saw that on top of that big, white, fluffy bed sat a big, white, fluffy cat.

"Meow?" said Mr. Nemesis. In cat language that means, "What do we have here?" or "My, don't you look delicious."

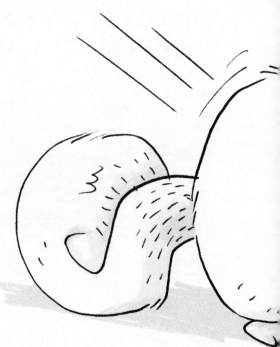

CHAPTER 7

"AHHHHH!" Merle screamed as he scrambled back to the air vent, his paws slipping on the wood floors.

Before he could reach the safety of the hole in the floor, Mr. Nemesis pounced onto the vent, blocking Merle's escape!

"AHHHHH!" Merle screamed again, turning to escape in the opposite direction.

In the quiet of Michael's room, Pearl heard a faint sound through the wall. She casually looked up from the math book and asked, "Merle? Did you say something?"

Meanwhile, Merle was running for his life! Feathers flew as Mr. Nemesis chased Merle over Jane's bed pillows, the cat's claws tearing the pillowcases and releasing their plumes. Merle dove into Princess Pretty-Pretty's castle and slipped out through the drawbridge as Mr. Nemesis landed on top of the main turret, causing the castle to topple over. Merle scurried under the bed as Mr. Nemesis regained his footing and followed. As Merle came out from under

the bed, he spotted the vent opening. The coast was clear! He made a mad dash, running faster than he had ever run in his life. Approaching his target, he leaped into the air and performed a perfect swan dive into the duct. Mr. Nemesis, so focused on catching Merle, failed to realize a cat is much too large to fit into a floor vent. The cat pounced high into the air and landed front paws and head first into the vent with a loud *THUMP!*

"MEOOOOOWWWWW!!!" yowled Mr. Nemesis, his head and front legs wedged into the vent, his back legs kicking wildly, trying in vain to free himself.

"YEE-HAW!!!" Merle yelled in relief as he scurried back through the vent toward Michael's room and safety.

CHAPTER 8

"Fractions! That's what you call them." Pearl pushed together two halves of a walnut. "Two halves of a nut equal one whole nut." Using her paws and repeating what she was learning out loud helped Pearl remember it.

"Pearl!" Merle popped his head out of the vent into Michael's room.

"AHHHHH!" yelled Pearl, startled. "Don't scare me like that!"

"Don't scare YOU like that?! I'm the one who was almost bitten in half!" Merle crawled up out of the grate, Mr. Nemesis's loud meows echoing from the floor vent.

"That's funny!" Pearl said. "I was just studying fractions."

"Yeah—hilarious," Merle responded sarcastically.

"How's the plan coming?" Pearl asked. "Did you find a place for us to live?"

"Nope," Merle said. "Unless you count inside a cat's stomach."

Just then, the door opened. Merle and Pearl were relieved to see that it was Michael, home from school. "Hey, guys, how was your day?" he asked.

"MEOOOOOWWWWW!!!" Mr. Nemesis's voice rang out.

Next came a shout from Jane: "MOOOOOM! Mr. Nemesis is stuck!"

"Coming, sweetie!" called Mrs. Gomez.

Michael shot Merle a questioning glance. Merle shrugged and smiled innocently.

"Well, Michael, are you ready to study for your math test?" Pearl asked. "I think I've got it figured out!"

Michael sighed and dropped his backpack on the desk. "I guess so."

CHAPTER 9

"Let's start with long division!" Pearl said cheerfully.

"You sound way too happy when you say that," Michael grumbled.

"What can I say?" Pearl grinned. "Math makes me happy!"

"Ugh!" Michael groaned as he plopped down next to Pearl at the desk. The two began studying. Pearl turned out to be a good teacher, and

Michael made some progress, but then he noticed his soccer ball sitting in the corner of the room.

"Where are you going?" Pearl asked as Michael stood up from his chair and walked toward the ball.

"You can ask me questions while I practice my foot-work." Michael began juggling his soccer ball.

Pearl frowned.

"I don't think you'll be able to concen-trate on your math while you're doing that."

"What?" Michael asked, distracted.

Merle, helping out, grabbed the ball as it left Michael's foot and pointed him back toward the desk.

"Ugh!" Michael repeated and plopped back down next to Pearl.

"All right. Maybe we should work a little on fractions?" she asked.

"Or maybe I can just eat a pound of raw brussels sprouts?" Michael said sarcastically.

"Ooh! That sounds delicious, but let's do fractions first," Pearl said.

Again, the two were making good progress, but before long, Michael was flat on his back on his bed, staring at the ceiling.

"Can you ask me questions while I lie here?" he asked.

"You can do this!" Pearl said, frustrated. "You just need to put more effort into it."

KNOCK! KNOCK! KNOCK!

Merle and Pearl scrambled to hide, but then they heard a familiar voice call through the door, "Can we come in?"

"Come on in!" Michael replied, and Justin and Sadie entered the room.

"I see you're studying hard!" Sadie said, noting the math book open on the desk.

"He could be studying harder," Pearl muttered.

"Well, we're done studying, and we wanted to celebrate by going roller-skating!" Justin said.

46

"Roller-skating?" Merle asked.

"It's where you put wheels on your feet and roll around," Michael explained.

"Why would you want to do that?" asked Merle.

"Because it's fun!" Sadie said.

"Well then, count me in!" Merle said. "It'll be nice to get out of the house."

"Great! Wanna come, Michael?" Justin asked.

"Michael, you still have to—" Pearl began to say, but Michael cut her off.

"I don't have any money to get in," he said.

"I can loan you the five bucks," Justin offered graciously.

Michael thought of the $10 bill waiting for him on the refrigerator. "Cool. Thanks, Justin. I can pay you back once I get a B on the test."

"I don't know if you are quite ready for the test," Pearl said. But

Michael was already on his feet and heading for the door.

"Hold on!" Pearl said. "Merle, do you remember the Thessalonians?"

CHAPTER 10

"Do I?!" Merle exclaimed. "Best baklava ever!"

"What's baklava?" Sadie asked.

"Nuts and honey on a light, flaky crust!" Merle licked his squirrel lips.

"Merle!" Pearl said. "Not the dessert—the people."

"Oh yeah. Them, too. Nice folks."

"Yes, nice, but some of them weren't the hardest workers," Pearl said. "Not long before our raft ride to the Dead Sea, the apostle Paul wrote a letter to the new Christians in Thessalonica. Some of the people in the church there had stopped working and were just taking it easy."

51

"Why's that?" asked Michael.

"Before he wrote the letter, a few years after Jesus' death and resurrection, Paul had visited the people in Thessalonica to tell them about what Jesus had done. He also told them that Jesus would be coming back soon," Pearl said.

"Some of them figured, 'Our troubles will be over soon, so why bother breaking a sweat? Might as well just relax!'" Merle said.

Pearl continued, "Paul told them, 'We hear that some of you are living idle lives, refusing to work and meddling in other people's business. We command such people and urge them in the name of the Lord Jesus Christ to settle down and work to earn their own living. As for the rest of you, dear brothers and sisters, never get tired of doing good.'"

Merle added, "That's not too different from what King Solomon said: 'Lazy people want much but get little, but those who work hard will prosper.' We're squirrels, so we should know. If we work hard collecting our nuts in the fall, we'll have a good winter."

"God wants us to work hard in serving him and others. That includes doing your best and studying hard in school!" Pearl concluded.

"I love that!" said Sadie.

"I couldn't agree more," added Justin.

Michael looked at his friends. "Are we going skating or what?"

CHAPTER 11

Merle and Pearl had never roller-skated before, for two reasons: (1) skates don't come in squirrel size and (2) skates weren't even invented until the 1700s. However, riding in the backpack of someone wearing roller skates can be just as much fun.

"Wheeeee!" Merle yelled as Michael made his way around the rink, loud pop music blaring, Justin and Sadie close behind. "This is amazing!"

"Merle, get down—someone's going to see you!" Pearl pulled Merle back down into Michael's backpack.

"I wanna skate!" Merle said. "I wanna skate like the wind!"

"They don't make skates in your size," Pearl reminded him.

"I'll make my own!" Merle responded. "Wheels for your feet! Why didn't I think of that?! Brilliant!"

The music changed to a slow ballad as a voice rang over the loudspeaker: "Okay, grab your sweetie. It's time for a couples' skate . . ."

Pearl noticed Sadie glancing over at Michael with a shy smile.

"Oh man!" Michael complained. "Not couples' skate!"

"Time for Skee-Ball!" Justin said.

Sadie shrugged and followed the

boys off the rink and onto the carpeted floor. Pearl couldn't help but think that Sadie looked a little disappointed.

"I'll make a pair of skates for you, too," Merle offered.

"Thank you, dear." Pearl squeezed his paw.

Merle thought Skee-Ball looked almost as fun as skating and begged the kids to let him try. To prevent other skaters from seeing Merle, Michael, Justin, and Sadie circled around the foot of the game to form a squirrel-obscuring human shield.

"Hrrrgh!!!" Merle grunted as he rolled the wooden ball up the track—and right into the gutter. However, after a few tries, he got the hang of it and started racking up points. By the time the couples' skate had ended and the kids were ready to return to skating, Merle had cashed out 150 tickets.

"What are these for?" Merle asked.

"You trade them in for toys," Michael told him.

"This is the happiest place on earth." Merle wiped a tear of joy from his eye.

CHAPTER 12

"Please put your book and all your notes away," Ms. McKay told the class. "It's time to start the test."

Michael swallowed hard. "Here we go . . ." He knew he should have stayed home and studied last night rather than go roller-skating, and now he was beginning to regret it. He didn't feel prepared for the test, but he was still hoping he might be able to squeak out a B. That way, he could collect his $10 reward and pay Justin back.

"Good luck!" Pearl whispered, popping up from his backpack. Since Jane didn't have preschool today,

Michael couldn't risk keeping the squirrels in his room, so he'd brought them to school with him again in his backpack.

"Thanks," Michael whispered back. He knew he would need it. Pearl ducked back down into the backpack as Ms. McKay walked by and placed Michael's test on his desk.

The first three questions were easy. Simple division—he remembered that from fourth grade. He breezed through them.

"Good job!" Pearl said.

"I think I'm gonna go grab some chicken nuggets," Merle said from the bottom of the pack. Merle and Pearl had collected an enormous amount of leftover food from the lunchroom a few days before.

"Don't overdo it!" Pearl warned. "Just a few."

"Got it!" Merle crept from the backpack and out of the classroom window, being careful to not be seen by Ms. McKay and the other students.

"Oh no," Michael whispered as he stared down at question 4.

Pearl peeked up at his test. Long division. She had helped Michael with a similar problem last night and knew exactly how to solve it. Pearl covered her face as Michael answered the question . . . incorrectly.

It was all downhill from there, and not in a good way. More in a way a train with no brakes runs downhill through a big pile of fractions and off a cliff. The answers were all painfully obvious to Pearl, who had put in the work of learning how to solve the problems. She sank back into the backpack with a groan as Michael stood up to turn in his test.

CHAPTER 13

"Hrrrgh!" *PLOP!* Merle slung a greasy brown paper bag onto the windowsill of Ms. McKay's classroom. Fortunately for Merle, the kids were reading their English assignment and Ms. McKay was grading tests, so nobody saw the squirrel making his way back into the room. He slid quietly back into Michael's backpack.

"I said just a few!" Pearl whispered as she noticed the size of the bag Merle was carrying.

"Sorry! I couldn't help myself. There were so many lost and lonely nuggets."

"They smell," Pearl complained.

"I know. Isn't it wonderful?" Merle took a big breath of deep-fried goodness.

"Okay, class. I have your tests for you," Ms. McKay said. "Some of you did very well. Congratulations! Some of you . . . well, we still have some work to do."

Merle and Pearl peeked their heads out of the backpack just in time to see Ms. McKay set Michael's graded test facedown on his desk. Michael looked down at the squirrels with a grimace before reaching to turn it over. "Well, here goes . . ." he whispered.

There's nothing that takes your breath away like getting a cold bucket of water dumped on your head, except for maybe seeing a big, red F on your math test. "What?!!!" Michael exclaimed, just as the bell rang and the kids gathered their things to leave for the day.

"Ohhhhh . . . Wow . . ." Justin said as he stood up and glanced at Michael's grade. "Sorry, dude."

"What did you get?" Michael wondered, hoping he was not alone in his grief.

"I did . . . okay," Justin said apologetically.

"Let me see!" Michael demanded.

Justin reluctantly showed Michael his test. A big, fat *A* with a smiley face covered the top.

"What?!!! No fair!" Michael griped.

"Michael, can I see you at my desk, please?" asked Ms. McKay. Michael sighed and stuffed his test in his backpack—covering Merle and Pearl—before zipping it closed and heading to the front of the class.

"Yes, ma'am?" Michael answered sheepishly as he approached Ms. McKay's desk.

His teacher gave him a stern look. "I know you can do better than this."

"Yes, ma'am," Michael agreed halfheartedly.

Ms. McKay folded her hands on top of her desk and leaned forward. "I'm going to make you a deal."

CHAPTER 14

"What did Ms. McKay say?" Sadie asked as the kids walked home from school.

"She told me I can take the test again," Michael answered. "She's giving me a second chance."

"That's great!" Merle said, his mouth full of chicken nugget. Merle was beginning to like going to school. Even if it meant spending most of the day crammed into a backpack, he could reward himself with chicken nuggets on the way home.

"Remember, Michael, if you work hard, you will prosper!" Pearl reminded him.

"I will, Pearl. Ms. McKay said the highest grade I can get on a retake is a B, but that's still a good grade," Michael said. "I'm ready to study hard!"

Just as Justin and Sadie were ready to break off to head to their own houses, a man in a suit and sunglasses, walking

a dog, approached the friends on the sidewalk. Something about him seemed odd to Michael. It was a cloudy fall day, the type of day when most people wouldn't be wearing sunglasses. Plus, who wears a suit when they walk their dog? Merle and Pearl ducked back into Michael's backpack as the two passed, the man's dog sniffing at the air. The dog began to bark, but the man said nothing and kept on his way.

"I think I've seen that guy somewhere before," Michael said quietly to his friends once the man and his dog were out of earshot, "but I can't remember where . . ."

"So, I did some research, Merle and Pearl," Sadie said, changing the subject. "You said you saw Jesus giving the Sermon on the Mount, which was around AD 27. And that you were around when Paul wrote his letter to the Thessalonians, which was sometime around AD 53. So, I'm guessing you must have gotten lost in that cave somewhere around AD 70."

"What year is it now?" Pearl asked.

"2020," Justin said.

"That's . . ." Pearl paused, then got an idea. "Michael, how many years since we got lost in the cave? Math question."

Michael thought a moment before

responding, "It was 1,950 years ago. 2020 – 70 = 1,950. That's easy. Just subtraction."

"We're off to a good start!" Pearl said.

CHAPTER 15

Michael entered the kitchen, where his mom and Jane were eating an after-school snack. "Cookies, would you like a cookie?" Mrs. Gomez asked.

"Mom!" Michael protested. "Don't call me Cookies! It's embarrassing!" Over the last year or so, he had grown to not like his mom's nickname for him.

"Oh, come on, it's cute. You're cute!" Mrs. Gomez offered him two cookies on a plate.

"I don't want to be cute! I'm in the fifth grade."

"You can be in the fifth grade and still be cute," his mom assured him.

As Michael reached for the cookies, Mr. Nemesis, who was perched
on top of the refrigerator, leaped onto
Michael's backpack. He had been waiting all day to get another chance at
the squirrel who had eluded him the
day before.

"MEOOOOOWWWWW!" Mr.
Nemesis growled, wiggling his head
into the partially unzipped top of the
backpack. Merle and Pearl found them-
selves face-to-face with the angry cat!
"MEOOOOOWWWWW!" Mr. Nemesis
said again, which in cat meant, "Aha!
I knew you were in here! I smelled you!"
The squirrels were trapped against the
bottom of the backpack, but thankfully,
the opening in the top was too small for
more than just Mr. Nemesis's head to fit
through.

"AHHHHH!" Merle screamed before Pearl put her paw over his mouth.

"Shhhhh!"

"Mr. Nemesis! Bad boy!" Mrs. Gomez shouted as she jumped up from the table to grab the cat. "What are you doing?"

Michael began spinning around, trying to fling Mr. Nemesis off.

"You're gonna make him fall!" Jane cried, worried about her cat.

"Good!" Michael said and spun faster.

Mrs. Gomez managed to stop Michael's rotation and grab Mr. Nemesis, yanking his head out of the backpack. "Naughty kitty!" she scolded. "Why in the world are you attacking a backpack?"

"Who knows?" Michael offered nervously. "Leftover chicken nuggets, maybe? Thanks for the cookies, Mom." Michael grabbed the cookies and set the plate down on the countertop by the refrigerator, noting the crisp $10 bill hanging from a magnet.

"Stay here and talk with us for a second," Mrs. Gomez called after him.

"Sorry, Mom. Can't! Gotta study!" Michael said as he headed for his room.

Mrs. Gomez smiled. "I won't argue with that."

CHAPTER 16

Although studying for a math test is a really important thing, reading about someone studying for a math test is a really boring thing, quite possibly the world's most boring thing. Suffice it to say that Michael studied hard. Even when he felt like giving up and juggling his soccer ball, or lying down on his bed, or playing video games, he pushed through and kept on going.

While Michael and Pearl worked on math, Merle worked on transforming one of Michael's dresser drawers into a cozy bed. "And it tucks away, too!" Merle said proudly, demonstrating the slider on the drawer.

"Great job!" Pearl told Michael and Merle as everyone turned in for the night. "We've all worked hard."

After a good night's sleep, Michael headed off to school in the morning, leaving his window open for Merle and Pearl.

As Jane left for preschool, Mr. Nemesis snuck out through her bedroom door, then outside through an open kitchen window. He watched as the squirrels exited Michael's bedroom window, and then he cleverly crept into Michael's room.

Merle and Pearl returned from gathering breakfast walnuts to find a crazed cat waiting for them.

"MEOOOOOWWWWW!" growled Mr. Nemesis, which in cat means . . .

"AHHHHH!" screamed Merle and
Pearl.

Fortunately, the squirrels were armed
with walnuts. As Mr. Nemesis pounced,
they pelted him with woody shells,
allowing them to make a break for
the air vent and scurry into the duct-
work. You would
think that Mr.
Nemesis would
have learned his

lesson about diving headfirst into a vent, but when a cat is focused on his prey, memory sometimes fails.

His head and forelegs once again jammed into a vent, Mr. Nemesis screamed out, "MEOOOOOWWWWW!" You don't want the translation for that.

CHAPTER 17

"Why is there a cat stuck in my floor?" Michael, back from school, looked around his room. Mr. Nemesis was the only animal in sight. "Merle? Pearl?" Michael whispered, concerned. Not hearing a response, he ran over and unplugged Mr. Nemesis from the vent. "What did you do with them?!" Michael demanded, holding the disgruntled cat at eye level.

"Grrrrr," Mr. Nemesis growled.

"Bad kitty," Michael scolded.

"We're in here!" Merle called out from the vent. Hearing Merle's voice, Mr. Nemesis tried to squirm free. Michael ran to the door and tossed him into the hallway, slamming his door shut before the cat could pounce back in.

THUD! "Mrrrrr!" could be heard on the other side of the door.

With the coast clear, Merle and Pearl popped their heads out of the vent.

"We have got to do something about these living arrangements," Merle complained.

"So? How did you do?" Pearl asked Michael eagerly.

Michael frowned. He reached into his backpack and pulled out a crumpled sheet of paper with a sigh.

"What?!" Pearl gasped. "I was sure that you—" She stopped as Michael handed her the test results. She stared at a big, fat 98 next to a big smiley face.

Michael cracked up. "Got you!" he said.

"Ohhhhh!" Pearl scowled. "Don't scare me like that!"

"It was a hard test, but studying paid off! Ms. McKay took 15 points off for the retake, which means I got

an 83—an official B! Now that $10 is mine, and I can pay Justin back with $5 to spare!"

"That's a lot of math right there," Merle noted.

"A good grade on your test is the best reward, but $10 is a nice incentive," Pearl said. "When you work hard, you prosper!"

"You know what this means, right?" Michael asked Merle. "Skee-Ball and skating to celebrate!"

"Woo-hoo!" Merle hollered. Michael and the squirrels circled up and did a happy dance in the middle of the room.

Suddenly, the door opened. Michael spun around to look, worried that Mr. Nemesis had figured out how to open it. No. Worse. Much worse. It was Michael's mom, staring in disbelief at her son happy dancing with two rodents. Justin and Sadie stood directly behind her, mouths hanging open.

"AHHHHH!!!" Mrs. Gomez screamed.

Before she could collect herself, Justin asked, "You guys ready to go skating?"

Michael knew he needed to act fast before his mom started asking questions. "Mom, can I go?"

Mrs. Gomez, in shock, simply nodded her head as Michael stuffed the squirrels into his backpack and headed out.

CHAPTER 18

Merle whooped as Michael leaned into the turn. "Faster!"

"Shhhhh!" Pearl said.

"No one can hear me, Pearl! The music's too loud!" Merle answered.

Justin and Sadie caught up to Michael. "Great job on your test, Michael!" Sadie said. Justin gave him a high five.

"It was hard work, but worth it," Michael replied.

"So, what are we gonna do now that your mom knows about the squirrels?" Justin asked.

"I don't know," Michael said. "I guess I'll find out tonight." He didn't want to think about it.

"Okay, skaters . . . it's time for a couples' skate!" the DJ announced as the music transitioned to a slow, romantic song.

"Oh, this is lovely," Pearl said. "Michael, can you stay on the floor so Merle and I can have this skate?"

"By myself?" Michael asked. "I can't couples' skate by myself!"

"I'll stay with you," Sadie offered, reaching out her hand.

"Ummm . . ." Michael stammered.

"Great!" Pearl exclaimed.

Michael, completely caught off guard, was too confused to take Sadie by the hand, something that all the other couple skaters (including Merle and Pearl) did. Instead, the two fifth-graders skated awkwardly next to each other to an Air Supply song.

As they rounded the bottom of the rink, passing the Skee-Ball machines, Sadie broke the uncomfortable silence. "Hey, Michael, it's that guy from your neighborhood!"

Michael looked over to see the man in the suit and sunglasses who they'd

seen earlier walking his dog. He
looked so familiar, but from where?
"Oh yeah!" Michael suddenly
recalled. "That's the
guy from the air-
port. What's he
doing here?"

MICHAEL GOMEZ is an adventurous and active 10-year-old boy. He is kindhearted but often acts before he thinks. He's friendly and talkative and blissfully unaware that most of his classmates think he's a bit geeky. Michael is super excited to be in fifth grade, which, in his mind, makes him "grade school royalty!"

MERLE SQUIRREL may be thousands of years old, but he never really grew up. He has endless enthusiasm for anything new and interesting—especially this strange modern world he finds himself in. He marvels at the self-refilling bowl of fresh drinking water (otherwise known as a toilet) and supplements his regular diet of tree nuts with what he believes might be the world's most perfect food: chicken nuggets. He's old enough to know better, but he often finds it hard to do better. Good thing he's got his wife, Pearl, to help him make wise choices.

PEARL SQUIRREL is wise beyond her many, many, many years, with enough common sense for both her and Merle. When Michael's in a bind, she loves to share a lesson or bit of wisdom from Bible events she witnessed in her youth. Pearl's biggest quirk is that she is a nut hoarder. Having come from a world where food is scarce, her instinct is to grab whatever she can. The abundance and variety of nuts in present-day Tennessee can lead to distraction and storage issues.

JUSTIN KESSLER is Michael's best friend. Justin is quieter and has better judgment than Michael, and he is super smart. He's a rule follower and is obsessed with being on time. He'll usually give in to what Michael wants to do after warning him of the likely consequences.

SADIE HENDERSON is Michael and Justin's other best friend. She enjoys video games and bowling just as much as cheerleading and pajama parties. She gets mad respect from her classmates as the only kid at Walnut Creek Elementary who's not afraid of school bully Edgar. Though Sadie's in a different homeroom than her two best friends, the three always sit together at lunch and hang out after class.

DR. GOMEZ, a professor of anthropology, is not thrilled when he finds out that his son, Michael, smuggled two ancient squirrels home from their summer trip to the Dead Sea, but he ends up seeing great value in having them around as original sources for his research. Dad loves his son's adventurous spirit but wishes Michael would look (or at least peek) before he leaps.

MRS. GOMEZ teaches part-time at her daughter's preschool and is a full-time mom to Michael and Jane. She feels sorry for the fish-out-of-water squirrels and looks for ways to help them feel at home, including constructing and decorating an over-the-top hamster mansion for Merle and Pearl in Michael's room. She also can't help but call Michael by her favorite (and his least favorite) nickname, Cookies.

MR. NEMESIS is the Gomez family cat who becomes Merle and Pearl's true nemesis. Jealous of the time and attention given to the squirrels by his family, Mr. Nemesis is continuously coming up with brilliant and creative ways to get rid of them. He hides his ability to talk from the family, but not the squirrels.

JANE GOMEZ is Michael's little sister. She's super adorable but delights in getting her brother busted so she can be known as the "good child." She thinks Merle and Pearl are the cutest things she has ever seen in her whole life (next to Mr. Nemesis) and is fond of dressing them up in her doll clothes.

DR. GOMEZ'S
Historical Handbook

So now you've heard of the Dead Sea Squirrels, but what about the **DEAD SEA *SCROLLS*?**

Way back in 1946, just after the end of World War II, in a cave along the banks of the Dead Sea, a 15-year-old boy came across some jars containing ancient scrolls while looking after his goats. When scholars and archaeologists found out about his discovery, the hunt for more scrolls was on! Over the next 10 years, many more scrolls and pieces of scrolls were found in 11 different caves.

There are different theories about exactly who wrote on the scrolls and hid them in the caves. One of the most popular ideas is that they belonged to a group of Jewish priests called Essenes, who lived in the desert because they had been thrown out of Jerusalem. One thing is for sure—the scrolls are very, very old! They were placed in the caves between the years 300 BC and AD 100!

Forty percent of the words on the scrolls come from the Bible. Parts of every Old Testament book except for the book of Esther have been discovered.

Of the remaining 60 percent, half are religious texts not found in the Bible, and half are historical records about the way people lived 2,000 years ago.

The discovery of the Dead Sea Scrolls is one of the most important archaeological finds in history!

About the Author

As co-creator of VeggieTales, co-founder
of Big Idea Entertainment, and the voice
of the beloved Larry the Cucumber,
MIKE NAWROCKI has been dedicated
to helping parents pass on biblical
values to their kids through storytelling
for over two decades. Mike currently
serves as Assistant Professor of Film and
Animation at Lipscomb University in
Nashville, Tennessee, and makes his
home in nearby Franklin with his wife,
Lisa, and their two children. The Dead
Sea Squirrels is Mike's first children's
book series.

WHAT'S THAT RACKET?

A cage door slamming, car tires squealing, and an elephant smashing to pieces! What are the Dead Sea Squirrels up to now?

Find out in
Squirrelnapped!

FOR ADVENTURERS

The Wormling series

Red Rock Mysteries series

FOR COMEDIANS

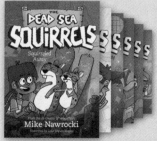

The Dead Sea Squirrels series

FOR ARTISTS

Made to Create with All My
Heart and Soul

Be Bold

FOR ANIMAL LOVERS

Winnie the Horse Gentler series

Starlight Animal Rescue series

CP1337